# Search for the Mermicorn

Swim into more

# PuRRMaiDS

adventures!

# PuRRmaids

4

## Search for the Mermicorn

### Sudipta Bardhan-Quallen
### illustrations by Vivien Wu

A STEPPING STONE™ BOOK
Random House 🏠 New York

Text copyright © 2018 by Sudipta Bardhan-Quallen
Cover art copyright © 2018 by Andrew Farley
Interior illustrations copyright © 2018 by Vivien Wu

Random House and the colophon are registered trademarks and A Stepping Stone Book and the colophon are trademarks of Penguin Random House LLC. PURRMAIDS® is a registered trademark of KIKIDOODLE LLC and is used under license from KIKIDOODLE LLC.

Visit us on the Web!
rhcbooks.com
SteppingStonesBooks.com

Educators and librarians, for a variety of teaching tools, visit us at RHTeachersLibrarians.com

*Library of Congress Cataloging-in-Publication Data*
Name: Bardhan-Quallen, Sudipta, author.
Title: Search for the mermicorn / Sudipta Bardhan-Quallen ;
illustrated by Vivien Wu.
Description: First edition. | New York : Random House, [2018]
Series: Purrmaids ; 4 | "A Stepping Stones Book."
Summary: As a school project, best friends and purrmaids
Angel, Coral, and Shelly set out in search of a mermicorn.
Identifiers: LCCN 2017030168 | ISBN 978-1-5247-0170-3 (trade pbk.) |
ISBN 978-1-5247-0171-0 (lib. bdg.) | ISBN 978-1-5247-0172-7 (ebook)
Subjects: | CYAC: Mermaids—Fiction. | Cats—Fiction. |
Unicorns—Fiction. | Narwhal—Fiction. |
Best friends—Fiction. | Friendship—Fiction.
Classification: LCC PZ7.B25007 Sdm 2018 | DDC [Fic]—dc23

Printed in the United States of America
10 9 8 7 6 5 4 3 2
First Edition

To Anika

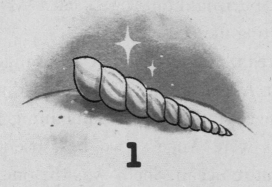

# 1

As far as Angel was concerned, room Eel-Twelve was the best place at sea school. Ms. Harbor, Angel's teacher, always made school paw-some. Every lesson since the first day had been filled with as much fun as facts. Each morning, Angel couldn't wait to get to class, because every day felt like it would be the best day ever.

"You're swimming too fast!" said a

white purrmaid on Angel's left. "My hair is getting messed up!"

"Yeah, Angel," panted an orange kitten on Angel's right. "Please slow down!"

Angel smiled. The complaining purrmaids were Angel's two best friends in the entire ocean. Shelly was the one with white silky fur. She was very picky about the way she looked and never wanted a single strand of fur out of place. Coral was the kitten with the orange fur. She was the smallest one in their group, and she didn't like having to swim twice as fast just to keep up.

Coral and Shelly were Angel's favorite things about Eel-Twelve. They were in the same class. That meant that Angel got to spend the entire school day with her best friends. What could be more purr-fect?

"I thought you both liked to be early for school," Angel teased.

"We can be early without swimming like a shark is chasing us!" Coral yelped.

"All right!" Angel laughed. She slowed down to let her friends catch up. "But we do need to hurry," she said. "I want to stop at the school library before we go to Eel-Twelve."

"Why?" Shelly asked.

"I have to get my book renewed," Angel replied. She pointed to a thick blue book in her bag. It was called *Legendary Creatures of the Purrmaid World,* and it was Angel's favorite book. "I want to read it again."

"Why didn't you just tell us you wanted to go to the library?" Coral joked. She loved reading. "That's a great reason to hurry!"

"We're almost there," Shelly said.

The girls swam straight to the library and hovered in front of the door. It was locked, and the school librarian, Mr. Shippley, wasn't there.

Angel stretched her neck to look through the window into Mr. Shippley's office. But all she saw was an empty room and the reflection of her black-and-white fur in the glass. "Where is he?" she asked.

Both Shelly and Coral shrugged.

Angel scowled. She needed the librarian to renew her book.

"The bell is about to ring," Coral said. "We have to get to class."

"Just put the book in the return slot for now," Shelly suggested. "We'll stop by after school so you can check it out again."

Angel didn't like that idea. But then

Coral said, "Come on, Angel. I don't want to be late!"

Coral always followed the rules, and that meant getting to Eel-Twelve on time. Angel sighed and dropped the book through the slot in the library door. Then she followed her friends to their classroom.

The girls arrived just in time for Ms. Harbor's announcement.

"Good morning, class," Ms. Harbor said. "Please get settled quickly. There are a few things we need to do before we go to the school library."

Angel's frown turned upside down. She didn't even have to wait until the end of the school day to check out her favorite book again!

"We've studied a lot of different things this year already," Ms. Harbor said. "We've learned about each other, about art, and about class pets. Today, I have a new project for you." She dimmed the lights and turned on the shell-ivision at the front of the room. "First, we're going to watch this fin-tastic video from the Kittentail Cove Science Center."

Everyone looked at the shell-ivision. The video showed different scientists discussing their jobs. One talked about trying to find ways to grow bigger and healthier sea vegetable crops.

"No!" Baker whined. "Who wants more vegetables?"

"Not me!" Taylor replied.

Another scientist's job was to track pollution. "I help the ocean stay clean," she said, "and keep dangerous trash away from animals like sea turtles."

"Now that's a good idea!" Shelly whispered. She loved sea turtles *and* ways to stay spotless!

A third scientist said he studied purrmaid history. "I've been reading the oldest books in Kittentail Cove. That way, we won't forget what we've learned from our past."

"That's the kind of job I'd like!" Coral said. She enjoyed reading more than anything in the ocean.

The last scientist said she kept records of all the animals around Kittentail Cove.

"I make sure they're healthy," she said. "Someday I hope to discover a new ocean animal."

Angel loved the sound of that.

When the video was over, Ms. Harbor asked, "What did you notice about the work these scientists talked about?"

Angel raised her paw. "They're all studying different things."

"Exactly!" Ms. Harbor said. "They find something fin-teresting—and they plan a research project around it."

The entire class nodded.

"These scientists inspired me," Ms. Harbor continued. "I know you are as curious as they are. I want you each to think about a special ocean animal. Then you're going to do a project about that animal."

"What kind of project?" Coral asked.

Ms. Harbor smiled. "That's the fun part! I'm not going to tell you what kind of project. You get to decide for yourself. There is only one thing you have to do. I'd like you to find at least one fact about your animal that most purrmaids don't know. Let's help each other learn something new!"

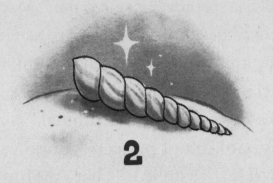

# 2

Ms. Harbor wasn't like most teachers at sea school. She had rainbow-colored fur, and she wore sparkly rings on her ears and her tail. But what made her so special wasn't her fur or her jewelry. It was that she didn't treat her students like little kittens who needed to follow instructions all the time. She always encouraged them to ask questions and to use their imaginations. Angel thought she was a paw-some teacher.

Most of Ms. Harbor's ideas made her students purr with excitement. But today, there weren't a lot of smiles. Baker and Taylor were both scratching their heads. The three girls in the Catfish Club—Umiko, Cascade, and Adrianna—had matching frowns on their faces.

Coral twisted the friendship bracelet on her paw over and over. That's how Angel knew Coral was especially worried. She only did that when she was nervous.

The bracelet Coral wore looked just like Angel's and Shelly's. The four charms on each bracelet reminded the girls of their adventures together as friends. The newest charm was a piece of sea glass. It made Angel think of Bubbles, the sea horse who she and her friends helped get back to his family.

Coral raised her paw to ask Ms. Harbor a question. "I don't really understand the project," she said. "Are we supposed to write a report? Or do a presentation? Or make a model?" She bit her lip. "Can we please have more instructions?"

Ms. Harbor floated over and patted Coral's shoulder. "As long as you pick a fin-teresting animal, I'm sure whatever you come up with will be purr-fect."

"But I don't know what animal to pick!" Coral sighed.

"Well," Ms. Harbor said, "it could be an animal we see all the time here in Kittentail Cove."

"Like Bubbles!" Shelly said. "I still visit him." She shrugged. "But I guess we already know a lot about sea horses."

"Yes," Ms. Harbor said. "Or it could be an animal we don't see very often."

"Like moray eels," Baker said.

"Or giant squids," Taylor added.

Their teacher nodded. "When you've picked an animal, I want you to study it," she continued. "You can observe the animal in the wild."

"But I can't go looking for giant squid!" Taylor yelped.

"Of course not," Ms. Harbor replied. "You can also read books at the library or talk to other purrmaids to get information."

Angel wasn't sure which ocean animal was her favorite. There were so many to choose from! But she already knew she wanted her project to be about one of the legendary creatures in her favorite book.

Angel wanted to leave for the library right away. But Adrianna asked, "What if we don't have a favorite animal?"

"Or what if we have too many favorite animals?" Cascade asked.

"Or what if our favorite animal is boring?" Umiko added.

Ms. Harbor threw up her paws. "You're worrying too much!" she said. "I know you all want to do a good job. I'm proud of you for that. But I want everyone to relax. I believe in each and every one of you, and

I know you're going to choose wonderful subjects." She swam to her desk and grabbed her notebook. "Now let's go to the library. I want you to put your energy into reading instead of worrying!"

The class lined up and headed down the hall. Angel swam next to Coral and squeezed her paw. "You heard Ms. Harbor," she whispered. "Don't fret! You always do well at school."

Coral flashed a little smile. "I just want to make sure I follow the rules," she said. "That's not so easy when there are none!"

"That just means we can make our own rules!" Shelly laughed. She loved rules when she thought of them herself.

"And," Angel added, "for once, you won't have to worry about me breaking them!"

All three girls giggled. Coral was the careful one in their group. Angel liked to dive first and worry later.

"The first rule I'm going to make," Shelly said, "is that we relax and try our best. I just know we'll find a way to help each other with our projects."

"We always do," Coral agreed.

"That's a rule even I can follow!" Angel exclaimed. "Now let's hurry and get to the library!"

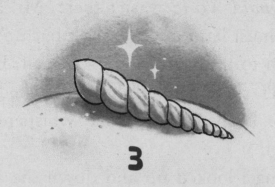

## 3

Mr. Shippley greeted the class at the school library. "Hello, Eel-Twelve!" he said. "Ms. Harbor told me about your project. I'm excited to hear your ideas."

Some students began to ask Mr. Shippley for help with their research. But Angel didn't have any questions. She knew exactly what she was looking for.

Angel checked the box near the librarian's desk. *Legendary Creatures of the*

*Purrmaid World* wasn't there. Mr. Shippley must have put the book back. Angel swam to her favorite book's shelf. But it wasn't there, either! She scratched her head. "Where is it?" she whispered to herself.

Angel looked up and down the aisles of the school library. She was trying to decide where to search next when a voice startled her.

"Hey, Angel!" Shelly called. Angel turned. Shelly was carrying a green book. She showed Angel the cover and said, "I found a great book about sea turtles."

"I knew they were your favorite!" Angel said.

"Did you find anything?" Shelly asked.

Angel shook her head. "I'm looking for the book I returned this morning," she said.

"I'll help you," Shelly said.

The two of them turned into the next aisle. But another student almost crashed right into them!

"Watch where you're swimming," Angel hissed. The purrmaid was holding a stack of books that was so tall it covered her entire face.

"I'm sorry, Angel," Coral said from behind the books. "I didn't see you."

"Of course you didn't!" Angel laughed. She wasn't surprised that Coral had found dozens of books before Angel had even found one. "Let us help you,"

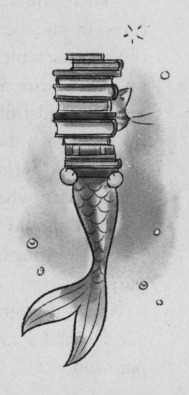

Angel said. She and Shelly each took a few books from Coral's pile. They swam over to the nearest table and put the books down.

"Wow, Coral," Shelly said. "You have lots of different topics here. How many projects are you planning to do?"

"There are just so many great creatures in the ocean!" Coral purred. "I can't decide which one to study." She held up a book with an orange cover. "I could make a model of a hammerhead shark," she said. Then she pointed to a gray book. "Or I could write a song and sing it like a humpback whale," she continued. "Or maybe I should write a research report on yellow tangs. They're so bright and purr-ty!"

Angel thought, *Coral has so many good ideas! I know her project will be paw-some.*

"Coral!" Shelly yelped. "I have a great plan! I was going to do a project on green sea turtles. Do you remember what Ms. Harbor told us about turtles and yellow tangs?"

"Yes," Coral answered. "They help each other on the reef."

Shelly reached for Coral's paws. "We could do our projects together," she suggested.

"And be a team just like green sea turtles and yellow tangs!" Coral exclaimed. They danced in a circle to celebrate.

"You should work with us, too, Angel," Shelly said. "It won't be the same without you."

Coral nodded. "Yellow tangs often swim near carnation corals," she said. "Maybe your project could be about those?"

The two girls smiled at Angel. But she

felt like frowning. She *always* wanted to work with her best friends. But carnation corals sounded so . . . *boring*. Even though schoolwork wasn't a contest, Angel really liked to be the best. She wanted her report to be the most fin-teresting one in the whole class!

Angel pawed through some of the books on the shelves. They were fin-teresting, but Angel didn't find a topic that was just right. *Any of the animals in my favorite book would be purr-fect for a project,* she thought. She really needed to find it!

Ms. Harbor let the class work in the library the whole day. When the dismissal bell rang, Angel jumped. Ms. Harbor shouted, "School's over, class! Good luck with your projects tonight."

Angel hung her head. "I didn't realize how much time had passed!" she cried. "I don't have my book yet."

"What are you going to do?" Shelly asked.

Angel shrugged. "I don't know," she said. She felt tears welling in her eyes. She blinked to hide them. Then she saw it.

There was something blue at the bottom of Coral's stack of books. Angel pulled it out. The bright gold letters on the cover spelled out *Legendary Creatures of the Purrmaid World.* "Here it is!" she gasped.

"Coral, you must have grabbed it with all the rest of these books!" Shelly said.

"I've been looking for this everywhere!" Angel yowled.

"Sorry, Angel," Coral said.

But Angel wasn't really listening. She was busy flipping pages. After a minute, she stopped. "Here!" she said. She turned the book and held it open for Shelly and Coral to see. "This is my favorite ocean animal. My project will be about mermicorns!"

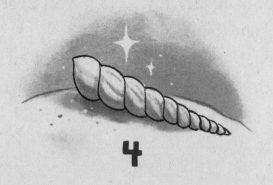

## 4

Angel was expecting her friends to be as excited as she was. But Shelly looked surprised, and Coral looked confused.

"What do you think?" Angel asked.

Shelly wrinkled her nose. "I guess it's a good idea," she answered.

Coral said, "I think Ms. Harbor wants us to pick a *real* animal for the project."

"Mermicorns *are* real!" Angel cried.

Coral bit her lip. "Have you ever seen one?" she asked.

Angel scowled. "No," she replied. "But that doesn't mean they don't exist. I've never seen a human, either. And I know they're real!"

Shelly giggled, but Coral frowned. "Even though *you've* never seen a human, other purrmaids have," she said. "I don't know anyone who has ever seen a mermicorn."

Angel looked down at the mermicorn drawing. The creature had the head and body of a horse with a rainbow mane. She had a tail that looked like a fish with rainbow scales, and she had a pearly horn on her head. Angel didn't want to think that something so beautiful was just make-believe. "Shouldn't we believe in things even if we can't see them?" she asked quietly.

Coral put a paw around Angel's waist and squeezed. "Maybe we should," she said, "but school is usually about things that we are sure are real."

"You're right about school, Coral,"

Shelly said. She hugged Angel. "But I think Angel is right, too. I wish there was a way to prove that mermicorns are real."

"What kind of proof are you looking for?" someone asked. Angel saw Mr. Shippley hovering nearby. "This is a library," he purred. "The shelves are filled with facts and evidence!"

Shelly held out Angel's book. "Can you show us another book about mermicorns?" she asked.

Mr. Shippley scratched his head. "That's a tough topic," he said. He took out a few books from a shelf near the table. "Look here."

The purrmaids swam closer. They saw a blurry picture of a creature halfway behind a large ocean rock. It looked nothing like any of the animals Angel had ever seen around Kittentail Cove. Its body was shaped a little like a dolphin but bigger. And it had a horn on its head—like a mermicorn! "What is that?" Angel asked.

Mr. Shippley shrugged. "A purrmaid family was on vacation in the Greenland Sea. They saw this creature and took a picture," he said. "They thought it was a mermicorn, but most scientists think it was a narwhal. Narwhals mostly live in cold water, so we don't see them very often."

"Could it be a mermicorn?" Angel asked.

"I suppose it *could* be," Mr. Shippley said. "Narwhals are sometimes called unicorns of the sea because of their long horns." He tapped a picture in another book.

This one showed the creature's horn very clearly, but the rest of the animal was completely covered by seaweed. "From time to time, there have been purrmaids who think they've found a true mermicorn, but we've never seen a clear picture. Some animals like to stay out of sight for their own safety. It's possible mermicorns do that."

The other photos showed more blurry creatures hovering behind or under something. They all had horns. But Angel didn't see hooves, manes, or anything else that looked like the mermicorn drawing until . . .

Mr. Shippley opened a small red book. When Angel looked carefully at the fuzzy photo, she saw something barely peeking out from behind a large piece of ice. There were lots of shadows, but Angel saw the creature's horn—and something colorful behind the horn! She flipped to the mermicorn drawing. "The mermicorn has a rainbow mane," she said. "And look here." She pointed. "Does it look like this drawing?"

Mr. Shippley held the two pages next to each other. He scratched his head. "I think that's probably just a trick of the light," he said. "Sometimes sunlight through the water looks like a rainbow."

Angel frowned. *It couldn't just be a trick, could it?*

Then Coral said, "I don't think it's sunlight, Mr. Shippley." She pointed to the ice. "Light wouldn't be able to go through ice that thick."

"So it *could* be a mermicorn mane!" Shelly exclaimed.

Mr. Shippley smiled. "Maybe," he said.

Suddenly, Angel thought of something. "Thank you, Mr. Shippley!" she said. She grabbed the red book and waved goodbye. Then she dragged Shelly and Coral around a bookcase.

"What are you doing?" Shelly yelped.

"You're messing up my fur! Why are you rushing us?"

"Remember the purrmaid from the video who said she wanted to discover a new ocean animal?" Angel said. Her friends nodded. "I think mermicorns are just waiting to be discovered. So that's what I want to do!"

"But how?" Coral asked.

Angel grinned. "I'll search all of Kittentail Cove," she replied.

Coral shook her head. "If there were mermicorns here," she said, "someone would have seen one already."

Coral had a good point. It wouldn't be enough to look around Meow Meadow or even Tortoiseshell Reef to find a mermicorn.

"I have an idea," Shelly said. "They work with sea turtles and yellow tangs at the Science Center. And they look for new ocean creatures. Maybe we can go there to work on our projects."

"That's a great idea!" Coral exclaimed. "And I have an idea, too. Let's do the project together. We'll all look for a mermicorn. Three pairs of eyes are better than one!"

"You two are paw-some!" Angel laughed. She began swimming to the door. "What are you waiting for?" she asked over her shoulder. "We need to get moving!"

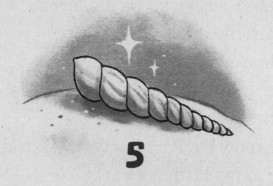

## 5

When the girls arrived at Angel's house, Mommy purred, "You must have raced here!" She winked. "I bet that means you're excited about something."

Angel grinned. Her mother knew her very well. "We have a new school project, Mommy," she said. "But we need more information than we could find at the school library." She held up the red book. "We'd like to look for a rare animal. Can we go to the Science Center this afternoon?"

Mommy scratched her head. "My friend Dr. Purrdew is the Science Center director," she said.

"I know Dr. Purrdew!" Angel said. "He came to my birthday party."

"Yes!" Mommy answered. She picked up her shell phone. "I'll call and ask if he can help you today."

Angel chewed her claws. She thought, *I hope Dr. Purrdew says yes.*

When Mommy hung up, she was smiling. Angel let out a deep sigh of relief. "Dr. Purrdew says he'd be happy to help three curious kittens with their research," Mommy said.

"Purr-fect!" Shelly said.

"Thank you!" Coral added.

"You can take the Cross Cove Current

west to the Science Center. Dr. Purrdew will meet you there," Mommy said.

Angel grabbed something from the kitchen drawer. "I'll take this to help us with the directions," she said. She held out a compass.

"Is that from the shipwreck we went to?" Shelly asked. The girls had explored a shipwreck at the beginning of the school year.

Angel nodded. "It could be useful!"

She tucked the compass and the red book into a small bag.

"Especially on our mermicorn search," Coral purred. "It can keep us from getting lost."

"Go ahead, you three," Mommy said. "You have lots to explore. Just make sure you stick together. Remember, you can always count on your friends."

Angel hugged her mother goodbye. "You're the best," she whispered.

🐾 🐾 🐾

The Science Center was on the far edge of Kittentail Cove. The town was on one side and a huge nature reserve was on the other. It would have taken hours for the purrmaids to swim there. Luckily, the Cross Cove Current ran through Kittentail Cove—and it was fast! Angel, Coral, and Shelly were able to ride it from

Angel's house all the way to the Science Center in just a few minutes.

The girls looked around for Dr. Purrdew. "Do you see him?" Coral whispered.

"No," Angel answered. She scanned the room. Dr. Purrdew was a gray-furred purrmaid who always wore a white lab coat and a pair of goggles. Angel couldn't see anyone dressed like that.

But she did spy someone else who looked familiar. It was the scientist from Ms. Harbor's video who wanted to discover a new ocean animal. Angel thought, *She might already be searching for mermicorns!*

"Hello!" Angel shouted. She waved.

The scientist swam toward the girls. "Can I help you?" she asked.

"I'm Angel, and these are my best friends, Shelly and Coral."

"We're students from sea school," Coral said.

"We need to learn about some ocean animals for a class project," Shelly added.

The scientist clapped her hands. "You've come to the right place!" she said. "I'm Pearl. I'm a student here at the Science Center."

"You're still in school?" Coral asked. "But you're a grown-up!"

Pearl laughed. "I'm not that grown up!"

"I see you already met one of my best students," said someone behind them.

Angel turned and saw gray fur and a white coat. "Dr. Purrdew," she said, "we were looking for you."

"I know!" exclaimed Dr. Purrdew. "Your mother says you want to explore the nature reserve."

"I can help you with that," Pearl said.

"Pearl knows the reserve like the back of her paw," Dr. Purrdew said. "She can take you anywhere. As long as the weather stays clear, it's safe for you to explore."

Angel twirled in the water. *Everything is working out purr-fectly,* she thought happily.

Pearl waved for the girls to follow her. "There's a fin-tastic place I think you girls would enjoy," she said. "There is a turtle-and-tang feeding-and-cleaning station in the east side of the reserve. It's in the area we call Firecracker Forest. We can observe the animals in their natural habitat."

Firecracker corals were bright orange. A forest of them would look dazzling. "That does sound fin-teresting," Angel said. "But we were actually hoping to find a different animal." She took a deep breath. "I know this is going to sound strange," she explained, "but we were hoping to find a mermicorn."

As soon as Angel said that, Pearl's smile disappeared. "A mermicorn?" she repeated. She shook her head. "I think that's going to be a purr-oblem."

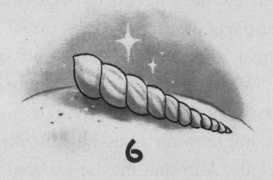

6

"First of all," Pearl said, "mermicorns are probably just animals called narwhals."

"We know," Coral replied. "They're called unicorns of the sea."

Pearl nodded. "The students here are careful about tracking the animals in the reserve," she explained. She opened a thick notebook on her desk. "I'm in charge of recording the sightings," she said. "We've seen a few narwhals here, mostly in the colder parts. But they're very rare."

Angel took the red book out of her bag. "We found this picture in our school library," she said. "We thought mermicorns might sometimes be mistaken for narwhals. And that maybe we could find one if we look hard enough."

Pearl studied the photo for a minute. "This looks like Siren Island," she said. She flipped through page after page in her notebook. "Once, a long time ago, a student reported seeing what he thought was a mermicorn up near Siren Island."

Angel felt butterfly fish fluttering in her tummy. Mermicorns might really exist! "Can we go to Siren Island?" she asked.

Pearl held up a paw. "No one else has ever seen what that student saw," she said. "I think it was probably just another narwhal."

Angel bit her lip. "We know it won't be easy," she said, "but maybe we'll get lucky today."

"Even if we don't find a mermicorn," Coral said, "we might be able to see a narwhal."

"And that would make a great project!" Shelly added.

Pearl took a map out of a desk drawer. She pointed to a spot on the map. "Here, directly to the north of Firecracker Forest, at the surface of the water, is Siren Island," she said. "It's actually an iceberg. It's cold up there."

"Too cold for purrmaids?" Coral asked.

"No, purrmaids can swim there," Pearl said. "All you need is a lab coat." She got three coats for Angel, Coral, and Shelly. She also grabbed three red buttons. They were marked with KITTENTAIL COVE SCIENCE CENTER—VISITOR. "If you're going out into the reserve with me, the rule is you need badges," Pearl said. She pinned a button on each coat. "There," she purred, "now you're allowed to explore everywhere."

"Purr-fect," said Coral. "I'm glad we won't be breaking the rules!"

"Come on!" Angel shouted. "Let's find a mermicorn!"

The purrmaids zipped through the ocean toward Siren Island. "We have to respect everything in the marine reserve," Pearl explained. "That means we don't touch anything we don't have to, and we make as little noise as possible."

"Why is that important?" Coral asked.

"That's a great question," Pearl replied. "We study ocean animals and plants to learn things that will help purrmaids everywhere."

"Like how to grow better sea vegetable crops," Shelly said. "We saw that in the Science Center video."

Pearl nodded. "But we also want to learn what our underwater neighbors need to be healthy and happy. For example, there are some animals who stay safe by keeping themselves hidden. Alligator pipefish look like pieces of sea grass. A lot of hungry predators ignore the pipefish because they don't want to eat a salad!"

"I don't blame them!" Coral laughed.

"If we poke around in a sea grass bed," Pearl continued, "we could drive the pipefish out into the open, where they could be eaten."

"So if an animal wants to stay hidden," Angel said, "we have to let them."

"Exactly," Pearl said. "The best way for purrmaids to help other animals is to learn what they need."

They reached Firecracker Forest. It was as fin-tastic as Pearl said it would be.

"Look at that!" Shelly whispered, pointing.

Three yellow tangs were cleaning a green sea turtle. "Amazing," Angel whispered.

"They work together as well as we do,"
Coral whispered.

Angel grinned. "You're right! There's
even one fish for each of us!"

"Here's another example of when purrmaids should know what the animals actually need," Pearl said. "Green sea turtles must have their shells cleaned to be able to swim easily. Purrmaids could go out and clean off their shells—but then a lot of yellow tangs would go hungry!"

"So by helping one creature," Angel said, "we could hurt another."

Pearl smiled. "You girls really understand how to be a good ocean neighbor," she said. They watched the feeding-and-cleaning station for a few minutes. Then Pearl said, "We should keep going. We're almost there."

Angel nodded. "Siren Island, here we come!"

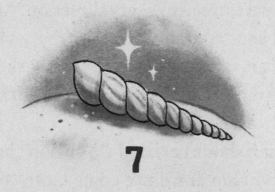

# 7

As the purrmaids got closer to Siren Island, the water became brighter from the sunlight. There were penguins swimming nearby, zipping over and under the surface of the water. But mostly, it was *cold*. "I'm so glad we have these coats," Angel said.

"When we get to Siren Island," Pearl said, "we can go up to the surface. That way we can see in every direction. Maybe we'll spot a mermicorn horn."

"Is it safe to do that?" Coral asked.

"Aren't there humans at the surface?" Shelly asked.

Pearl shook her head. "You don't have to worry. Humans don't come close enough to Siren Island to be a purr-oblem."

Soon Angel could see the underwater part of Siren Island. It was like a huge mountain of ice. But instead of growing tall toward the sky, the ice stretched down toward the ocean floor. Seals and penguins swam into tunnels snaking through the ice.

Pearl moved to the surface and poked her head out of the water. She waved for the girls to do the same. "It's beautiful up here," she sighed.

Most purrmaids spent their lives deep

under the sea. So Angel, Shelly, and Coral hadn't ever been to the surface of the ocean. They never could have imagined what they saw. The iceberg itself was about as big as Meow Meadow. The ice was so bright that it looked like it was glowing against the blue of the sky.

Underwater, there were always animals or seaweed that blocked the view. But the air above Siren Island was completely clear. "I can see all the way to the other side of the island!" Angel exclaimed.

"I know!" Pearl laughed. "It's so different from being deep in the ocean!"

The purrmaids sat on the edge of Siren Island with their tails dipped in the water. The sun was shining brightly. Angel shielded her eyes with a paw and looked all around. She saw a pod of killer whales on the northern side of the iceberg. Coral spied a humpback whale swimming to the south. Shelly spotted a gathering of puffins plopping into the sea on the eastern side. Pearl thought she saw a sea spider to the west—but it was just some seaweed.

None of them saw anything that looked like a narwhal or a mermicorn.

After a while, Shelly said, "It's getting late, Angel." She pointed to the sky. The sunshine wasn't as bright. In fact, there were dark clouds gathering. "This was a good plan, but it might not work out the way we wanted."

"Maybe we should go back to the feeding-and-cleaning station," Coral said. "I don't want to get in trouble for not finishing our project."

But Angel wasn't ready to leave. She strained to see something—anything—in the distance.

Suddenly, she shouted, "Look!"

"What is it?" Pearl asked.

Angel waved her friends over with one paw and pointed with the other. "I think I found something!" she gasped.

There were four horns poking out of the water on the far side of Siren Island.

"We have to move closer," Angel said.

"And we have to hurry!" Shelly added.

The purrmaids raced toward the horns.

When they reached the other side of Siren Island, Angel gasped. "I see them! I see them!"

"Where?" Pearl asked.

Angel pointed at a patch of water near the iceberg. It was partially surrounded by smaller icebergs, creating a private pool. There were narwhals gathered there, splashing in the sunlight. They were huge! Most of them were longer than a dozen purrmaids lined up.

"I've read about narwhal pods," Pearl whispered, "but I never knew there could be this many narwhals in one place!"

"There must be at least twenty," Angel said. Then she realized something. "They don't all have horns!"

"That's true," Coral said. "Only about half have horns."

"It must be a difference between males and females!" Pearl exclaimed. "That happens with a lot of animals. But no one knew that about narwhals."

"We made a discovery!" squealed Shelly. "That's fin-tastic!"

"Dr. Purrdew will be so excited about this," Pearl said.

"So will Ms. Harbor," Coral added.

Then Angel spied something else. "Look over here!" she yelped. "I think it's a baby narwhal." She pointed at a smaller creature who looked a lot like a big narwhal. The baby noticed Angel and playfully splashed water at her. She giggled.

"He's so cute!" Shelly said. "Let's swim with him."

"I don't think we should," Angel said. "Narwhals aren't used to purrmaids. We don't want to scare him or his parents."

"Angel's right," Pearl said. "We can

observe the narwhals to learn about them. If they come to us like this little guy did, it's fine. But we shouldn't do anything to disturb them."

"That makes sense," Coral said. Shelly nodded.

The purrmaids watched the narwhals swim around the iceberg. "What an amazing day," Angel purred.

"I just wish we'd found a mermicorn, too," Shelly said.

Angel shrugged. "That would have been great," she said.

"We didn't find mermicorns," Coral said, "but we did make a wonderful discovery about narwhals."

Pearl said, "I'm so glad you girls convinced me to come to Siren Island."

Angel smiled as the narwhals swam

out of sight. When she felt some drops of water, it surprised her. "Someone is splashing me!" she yowled.

"Is it the baby narwhal again?" Shelly asked. But all the narwhals were gone.

"I don't think anyone is splashing," Coral said. She pointed up at the sky. A huge rain cloud had drifted above Siren Island. "I think we have a different purr-oblem."

Soon the sun was completely blocked. Bigger drops began to fall.

"It's raining!" Shelly exclaimed.

Then there was a crash of thunder. A moment later, a streak of lightning lit up the sky. Shelly and Angel flinched. "What was that?" Coral yelped.

"It's not just rain," Pearl shouted. "It's a thunderstorm!"

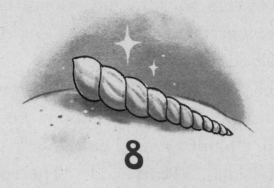

# 8

Usually, rain in the skies above didn't affect purrmaids. After all, the ocean couldn't get much wetter! But thunderstorms were a different story. Weather that bad could cause powerful waves, which made swimming near the surface dangerous. And lightning was very serious. A purrmaid who was struck by lightning could be badly hurt.

"Let's go back to the Science Center before it gets worse out here," Angel said.

"Good plan," Pearl replied.

The purrmaids dived into the water. The ocean was already choppy from the storm. "I think we should swim under Siren Island," Pearl said. "The tunnels through the iceberg won't be as rough. They can get a little confusing, so try to stay close."

The girls followed Pearl through the nearest tunnel. The water there was calmer but still rough. Every once in a while, a wave would crash into one of the purrmaids and knock her against the ice. Since Coral was the smallest, she had the hardest time.

There was a clap of thunder, and then a giant wave came down the tunnel.

"Quick!" Pearl shouted. "Turn here!" She darted into another tunnel.

Shelly and Angel were about to turn when they heard a yelp. "Ouch!" Coral cried. The ocean was knocking her around again.

"We have to help her!" Angel yelled.

They fought through the waves to reach their friend. "We've got you, Coral," Shelly called.

"Hold on to each other," Angel said. She held one of Coral's paws, and Shelly held the other. "We can make it to the next tunnel if we swim together."

Angel moved forward. But she had a hard time staying on course because of the waves. And she couldn't figure out where to turn to find Pearl.

Luckily, she heard Pearl's voice. "Girls, are you all right?"

"We're coming!" Angel replied.

"The water is much calmer in this tunnel!" Pearl shouted. "As soon as you turn, you'll be fine!"

"Follow Pearl's voice," Angel said. "I think she's over there on the left."

The three girls fought their way forward. Finally, they turned left. As soon as they were in that tunnel, the water completely changed. Now it was still. The girls leaned against the ice wall to rest for a moment.

"We made it," Shelly panted.

"Thanks for coming to help me," Coral said.

"Of course!" Angel said. "You're our best friend!"

The purrmaids smiled at each other. Then Angel said, "Where's Pearl?"

"Angel? Shelly? Coral?" said Pearl. "I can hear you, but I don't know where you are!"

"She sounds so close," Shelly said, "but I don't see her."

"I think she's on the other side of the ice!" Angel exclaimed. She pointed. A Pearl-shaped outline swam along the wall of the tunnel.

"We're over here!" Coral shouted. "But you're in a different tunnel."

"All right, wait there!" Pearl yelled. "I'll go back and find the tunnel you're in."

"You can't!" Angel said. "The water is too dangerous back there. You could get hurt."

"But how will you three get back to the Science Center?" Pearl asked.

"I don't know the way," Shelly said.

"Neither do I," Coral added.

Angel scratched her head. Then she remembered. "The compass!" she yelped. She took it out of her bag. "Pearl," she shouted, "did you say that Siren Island is north of Firecracker Forest?"

"Yes," Pearl answered.

"Then we can use my compass to swim south from here!" Angel said.

"That's a great plan!" Shelly squealed.

"Are you sure you'll be all right?" Pearl asked.

"We'll stick together," Angel said, "and we'll meet you at Firecracker Forest."

"Then we can go to the Science Center together," Coral said.

Pearl shouted, "Please be careful!"

"We will!" Angel yelled.

The girls swam through the tunnel away from the storm. There were lots of twists and turns, but Angel kept checking the compass. "We're still headed south," she said.

After a few minutes of swimming, Angel said, "Hurry! I see the end of the tunnel." The purrmaids moved toward the opening. That's when Angel shrieked. "I can't believe it!" she said.

"What?" Shelly asked. As soon as she

saw what Angel was pointing at, her jaw
fell open. She stammered, "Is—is that—?"

Now Coral was looking in that direction. "A mermicorn?" she asked.

"Please don't hurt me!" gasped the
mermicorn.

9

The creature floating in front of the purrmaids looked like a white horse with a rainbow mane. But she didn't have back legs like a horse. Instead, she had a glimmering fish tail.

Angel saw how scared the mermicorn looked. "We won't hurt you," she purred.

"We've been searching all over the ocean for you!" Coral exclaimed.

"Why would you do that?" the

mermicorn asked. "I don't even know you."

"Because we wanted to prove that mermicorns are real," Shelly said.

"Of course I'm real," the mermicorn said.

"We didn't know that. Purrmaids think you're just make-believe," Angel said.

The mermicorn snorted. "Well, my mother told me creatures that are half-cat and half-mermaid are just make-believe," she replied.

Coral laughed. "I guess we discovered you, and you discovered us!"

Angel swam closer to the mermicorn. "I'm Angel," she said. "What's your name?"

The mermicorn shyly held out a hoof to Angel. "I'm Sirena," she said.

"These are my friends Shelly and

Coral," Angel said, pointing to the other purrmaids.

"You don't seem scary," Sirena said.

"We're not!" Shelly said.

"When I get home to Sea Dragon Bay," Sirena said, "I'm going to tell my friends and family about you." But then she frowned. "*If* I ever get home, that is."

"What do you mean?" Coral asked.

Sirena sighed. She waved for everyone to follow her, then she swam through the tunnel opening. "Do you see that kelp forest?" she asked.

The purrmaids nodded.

"I know Sea Dragon Bay is on the eastern side of that forest," Sirena said. "But when I got stuck in the storm, I got all turned around. Now I'm lost!"

"We're on our way back to our home,

Kittentail Cove," Angel said. "There are maps there, and our friend Pearl could help you find Sea Dragon Bay."

"Yes!" Shelly said. "Come back with us. We want everyone to meet you."

"That way they'll know that mermicorns are real," Coral said.

Sirena shook her head. "I can't come with you," she mumbled.

"Why not?" Angel asked.

"Mermicorns like to stay out of sight," Sirena replied. "We're not the fastest swimmers in the ocean. Our horns are just there to be pretty. We can't use them to defend ourselves. So staying hidden is how we keep ourselves safe. We mostly remain in Sea Dragon Bay. Out in the rest of the ocean, we keep to the shadows."

Angel remembered something. She

opened the red library book to the mermicorn picture. "You mean you hide like this?" she asked.

Sirena looked at the photo. "That looks like my uncle Hudson," she said.

"You were right, Angel!" Shelly said. "That *is* a mermicorn!"

"I don't think the other mermicorns at home would want everyone in the ocean to know about us," Sirena said. "Besides, our town won't be on any of your maps. Only mermicorns know about Sea Dragon Bay."

Angel looked out at the kelp forest. "Did you say Sea Dragon Bay was on the east side of the forest?" she asked.

Sirena nodded.

"Then we can get you home!" Angel cried.

"How?" Sirena gasped.

Angel held up her compass. "By using this," she replied.

"I don't understand," Sirena said.

"This is a compass," Angel said. "It helps you find your way around the ocean." She placed it on her paw and watched the needle spin. "That way is north," she said, pointing.

Shelly pointed the other way. "Which means that is south," she said.

"If that's south," Coral added, "then east is this way." She turned left and pointed.

Sirena reached for the compass. "This is fin-credible," she said. "It always points north? Even in a dark kelp forest? Or in a thunderstorm?"

Angel nodded. "Take it," she said. "That way you can find your way back

to Sea Dragon Bay. And you won't have to worry about getting turned around again."

"But then how will you three get home?" Sirena asked.

"Well, south is that way," Angel said. She turned and strained to see into the distance. She could just make out bright orange-and-yellow corals. "That's where Firecracker Forest is."

"Pearl will be waiting there," Shelly said. "She'll take us the rest of the way home."

"Since we can see it," Coral added, "we can swim there easily."

"There's no kelp to get lost in," Angel said, "so we won't need the compass."

Sirena grinned. Then she hugged each of the purrmaids. "Thank you," she whispered. "I guess it was lucky that I got lost today. Otherwise, I wouldn't have found something wonderful—new friends."

😺 😺 😺

As soon as Sirena was on her way, the purrmaids left for Firecracker Forest. They hurried so Pearl wouldn't worry.

"I can't wait to tell Pearl about Sirena!" Coral said as they swam.

Angel shook her head. "I don't think we should say anything," she said.

"Why not?" Shelly asked. "You were the one who wanted to discover a mermicorn. Why wouldn't we tell Pearl that that's what we did?"

"Sirena said that mermicorns feel safe when they're hidden," Angel said. "If we tell Pearl about her, won't Dr. Purrdew and the other scientists want to find her and Sea Dragon Bay?"

"Maybe," Coral said. "But why would that be bad?"

"Mermicorns don't have to be afraid of purrmaids," Shelly added.

"No, they don't," Angel agreed. "But I think it should be their choice, not ours." She turned and looked back. Sirena was about to enter the kelp forest. "Sirena knows how to find us. If the mermicorns want to, they'll come to Kittentail Cove. We can be good ocean neighbors by doing what's best for the mermicorns."

"You're right," Shelly said.

"I guess this means we won't tell the class about mermicorns tomorrow," said Coral.

Angel smiled. "I think we should talk about the narwhals we found," she said. "They were very fin-teresting."

"That's purr-fect," Shelly agreed.

*And this* was *the best day ever,* Angel thought.

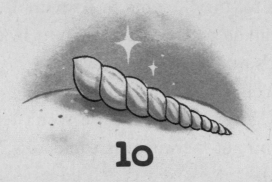

## 10

In the morning, Angel was so excited about sea school that she got to Leondra's Square before either of her best friends. She was holding a large picture of narwhals. She had painted it the night before to share with the class.

"That looks great, Angel," Shelly called as she and Coral swam up.

"We don't have time for compliments!"

Angel replied. "I want to get to Eel-Twelve quickly!"

Coral laughed. "How did I know you'd be in a hurry?"

For the second day in a row, the girls got to sea school early. Angel squirmed in her clamshell seat—she could hardly wait for the morning bell!

When Ms. Harbor saw Angel's painting, she exclaimed, "That's beautiful!"

"Thank you!" Angel said. "It's part of our project on narwhals. We found a whole pod in the nature reserve at the Science Center."

"I'll bet it was quite an adventure," Ms. Harbor said.

The bell rang, and everyone took their seats. Angel was about to ask Ms. Harbor if she, Shelly, and Coral could present their project first. But Shelly spoke before Angel could.

"Ms. Harbor," said Shelly, "Coral and I would like to share our project first."

Angel frowned. *It's my project, too,* she thought. How could her best friends have forgotten about her?

But when she tried to go to the front of the class, Coral said, "Your project is about narwhals. Shelly and I have a different project."

Angel froze. "I don't understand," she said.

"You will soon," said Shelly.

"In just a few minutes, Angel is going to tell us all about the narwhals we saw yesterday at the Kittentail Cove Science Center," Coral began. "I didn't know if we'd find any because they're so rare."

"Angel was the one who had faith,"

Shelly said. "Coral and I decided that Angel should really get the lionfish's share of the credit for that."

"No!" Angel gasped. "We all worked together!"

Shelly and Coral shook their heads. "We helped you, Angel," Coral said, "but it was *your* project."

"We may have all explored Siren Island together," Shelly said, "but without Angel, we never would have discovered all the things we did." She winked at Angel.

"That's why Shelly and I decided that we wanted to share another project today," Coral said. "We'd like to tell you about another fin-credible ocean animal."

Angel felt her cheeks grow hot. She couldn't believe it! Coral and Shelly were going to tell everyone about Sirena!

Before Angel could say anything, Shelly continued, "This ocean animal is someone who never gives up. She's curious and brave, and she's always ready for anything new and exciting."

"She's fearless in thunderstorms," Coral said.

"And she cares about her friends," Shelly added. "Even the ones she's just met."

Suddenly, Angel knew exactly who her friends were talking about.

"This paw-some ocean animal," purred Coral, "is our friend Angel."

Angel kept opening her mouth, but no words came out. Shelly and Coral didn't seem to care. They swam to Angel's seat and hugged her. The entire class clapped.

"We have one more thing for you," Shelly whispered. She held something out in her paw. It was one of the red Science Center buttons.

"We thought these would make great charms for our friendship bracelets," Coral said. She and Shelly raised their paws to show that they'd already added their red buttons.

Angel added the button to her bracelet. It looked purr-fect next to the sea-glass charm. "Thank you," she said. "I love it!"

"Wonderful job!" Ms. Harbor exclaimed. "Thank you, Coral and Shelly." She turned to Angel. "Now I'd like to hear about these narwhals. Angel,

would you like to share your project next?"

Angel nodded. "It all started with a great library book," she began. She carried her painting to the front of the room and grinned one more time at Shelly and Coral.

The students of Eel-Twelve leaned forward, ready to hear about the whole adventure. "Don't keep us waiting!" Ms. Harbor said.

Angel smiled. "It's a long story so you have to be a little patient," she purred, "but I promise, you'll love the ending!"

# New friends. New adventures.
# Find a new series . . . just for you!

ISADORA MOON

COMMANDER IN CHEESE

JULIAN'S WORLD
THE STORIES JULIAN TELLS

For ballerina and fairy and vampire lovers

For adventurers

For storytellers

PUPPY PIRATES

PURRmaids

BALLPARK Mysteries

For dog lovers

For mermaid and cat lovers

For sports fans

**RHCBooks.com**

1220a